W9-BKE-923

GRIZZLY
BOY

little bigfoot
an imprint of sasquatch books
seattle, wa

BARBARA DAVIS·PYLES

illustrated by TRACY SUBISAK

One morning, Theo decided
he was no longer human.

Theo leaped out of bed.

Then he practiced his growl . . .

GRRROWLLLLLL

his roar . . .

ROARRRRRRRR

Oh my!

and scratching his bottom on the bedpost. But then . . .

Theo let his skivvies fly.

His mom flung the windows wide open so he could feel the forest breeze.

He reached for his briefs.

But then . . .

Theo tossed his shoes out the window and stomped off to breakfast with his big bare feet. But when . . .

he looked into his bowl, he did not see Frosted Monster Bites. He saw lettuce and berries and mushrooms and sprouts!

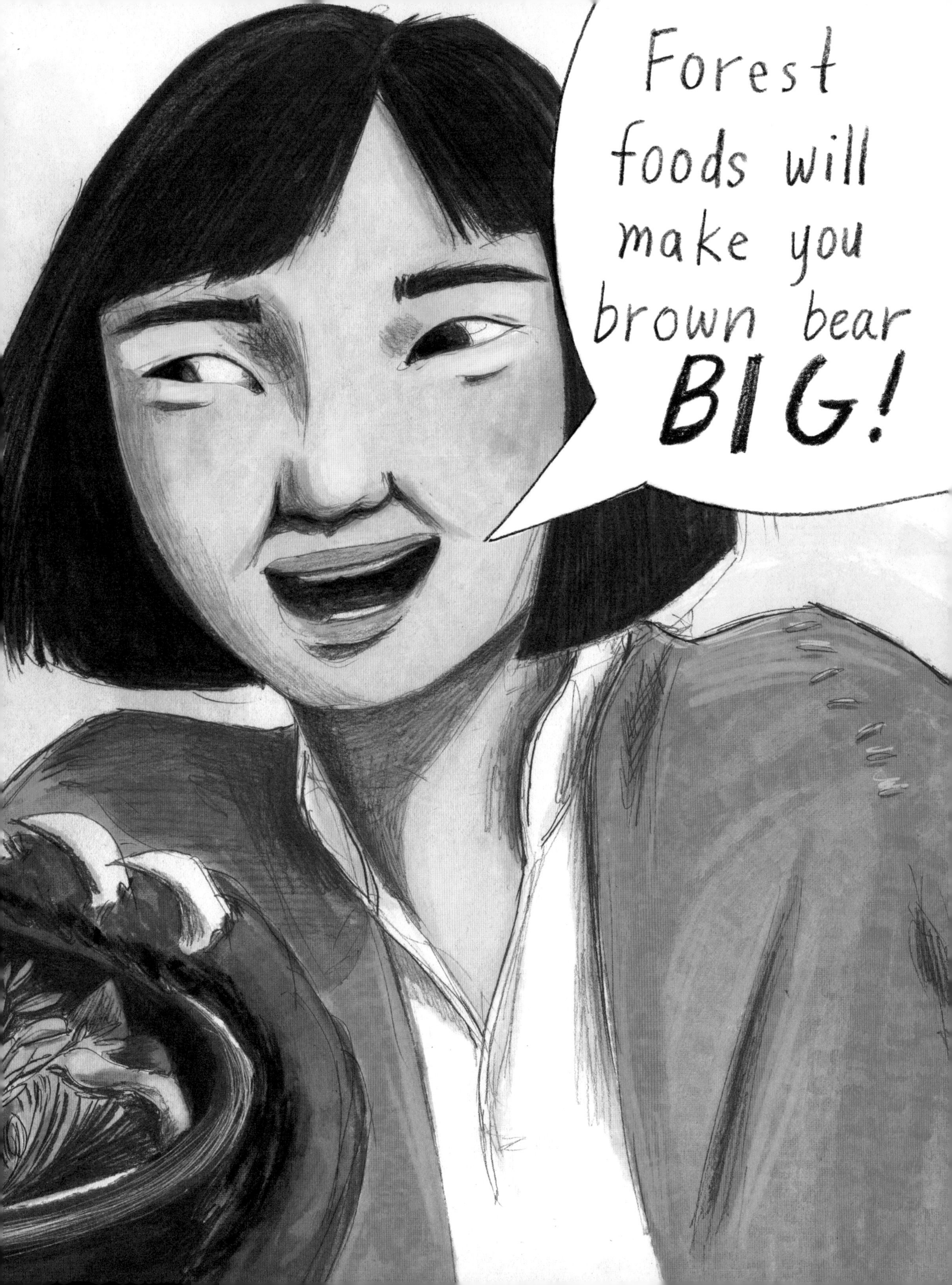
Forest foods will make you brown bear BIG!

Theo had a frightening thought. *If there aren't Frosted Monster Bites in the forest, there probably isn't ice cream either.*

But then . . .

RAWR!

Theo ran off to fire up his Supersonic-Smash Storm Racer game.

But a supersized sign stopped him in his tracks!

Theo lumbered off to school with his big bare feet.

School was chock-full of
RULES, RULES, RULES!

There were rules about chairs!

There were rules about lines!

There were rules about books and pencils and paste! There were even rules about shoes!

And so . . .

all of the humans went out for recess, wild and free, while Theo wrote apologies (with no help at all from his imaginary fleas).

His mom didn't say anything. She just frowned into the soup she was stirring. But suddenly . . .

she let her spoon soar!

And so . . .

they both tossed their shoes out the window. Then they ran to the park with their big bare feet and played for hours . . .

wild and free.

For Grace and Christopher
my wild and wonderful cubs — Barbara

To 媽媽。好想你啊~ —T

Manufactured in China by C&C Offset Printing Co. Ltd. Shenzhen,
Guangdong Province, in May 2018

Published by Little Bigfoot, an imprint of Sasquatch Books

22 21 20 19 18   9 8 7 6 5 4 3 2 1

Editors: Christy Cox, Ben Clanton
Production editor: Em Gale
Design: Anna Goldstein

ISBN: 978-1-63217-168-9

Library of Congress Cataloging-in-Publication Data
    Names: Davis-Pyles, Barbara, author. | Subisak, Tracy, illustrator.
Title: Grizzly boy / Barbara Davis-Pyles ; illustrated by Tracy Subisak.
Description: Seattle : Little Bigfoot, [2018] | Summary: Tired of rules, a
    young boy decides to be a wild and free bear but soon runs into obstacles.
Identifiers: LCCN 2018000268 | ISBN 9781632171689 (hardback)
Subjects: | CYAC: Grizzly bear--Fiction. | Bears--Fiction. |
    Imagination--Fiction. | Rules (Philosophy)--Fiction. | BISAC: JUVENILE
    FICTION / Nature & the Natural World / General (see also headings under
    Animals). | JUVENILE FICTION / Animals / Bears. | JUVENILE FICTION /
    Family / Parents.
Classification: LCC PZ7.1.D355 Gr 2018 | DDC [E]--dc23
LC record available at https://lccn.loc.gov/2018000268

SASQUATCH BOOKS
1904 Third Avenue, Suite 710 | Seattle, WA 98101
(206) 467-4300 | SasquatchBooks.com

BARBARA DAVIS·PYLES lives wild and free in the northwest corner of Washington State. Sometimes she even makes dinner.

TRACY SUBISAK lives in Portland, Oregon, and can often be found traveling the world. She is fond of hiking, bacon, monster sounds, and high fives!